FUTURE

FLASH

FUTURE

FLASH

**Seventeen
Selected Semi-
Serious Short-
Short Science
Fiction Stories
& Several
Shameless Sets
of Sententious
Stanzas**

by

Arlan Andrews, Sr.

Founder of SIGMA, the Science Fiction Think Tank[TM]

Hydra
Publications

Printed in the United States of America

ISBN: 978-1-942212-55-3

Carbon Zero (Visions 2100 anthology, December 2015)
War, With Incident (Baby Shoes anthology, September 2015)
Foundation and Zombies (Stupefying Stories Showcase, November 2014)
Wreck Support (Analog, September 2013)
...Plus C'est Le Meme Chose (Analog, July/August 2011)
Pilots of the Purple Twilight (story to United States Dept. of Homeland Security, 2010)
What Engineers Know (Analog, November 2004)
2020: The Chimera Engineer (Virtual Manufacturing Proceedings, University of New Mexico Press, March 1995)
Rite of Privacy (Amazing Stories, January 1989)
A Visit to the Nanodentist (Amazing Stories, May 1989)
The Mars Farewell (Amazing Stories, May 1989)
Mystery of the Space Pirates (Pulsar!, October 1988)
Snuff (Lan's Lantern, August 1988)
Fantasy of a 50's Fan (Amazing Stories, July 1988)
Surfaced Tension (Analog, January 1988)
Occidental Injury (Analog, October 1987)
QTL (Analog, February 1987)
Information Implosion (Analog, mid-September 1983)
Making sure the OCTOPUS is kept at arm's length (Infoworld, April 4, 1983)
Ozma, Revisited (Cosmic Search, Spring 1981)
Rime of the Ancient Engineer (Isaac Asimov's Science Fiction Magazine, January 1980)

Hydra Publications
1310 Meadowridge Trail
Goshen, KY 40026

Table of Contents

<u>Comments on the Work</u>

I've been writing short science fiction for a long time. Invariably, the question arises, "Where can I find your stories?" Being that it is increasingly difficult (and expensive) to locate old science fiction magazines, not to mention the more obscure publications – computer trade magazines, no-longer-published sources, various specialty items, etc. – I decided to retrieve some of those stories that have not otherwise been anthologized, with a few exceptions. Other volumes will follow.

The stories in this Volume range from very short to merely short, a venue I relished writing in over the years, especially those for the *Probability Zero* section of *Analog*, where seven of these flashes first appeared.

By necessity, short fiction focuses on very specific actions and actors, so that humor, puns, tricky punch lines, shaggy dog stories, all make their appearances here. In reality, these mini-stories are my homage to the truly great science fiction writer Frederic Brown, master of what is now called "Flash Fiction." He was an early inspiration.

The entries in the Table of Contents are arranged chronologically, from the latest in 2015, all the way back to my first paid publication, a poem, in 1980.

[Author's Comments: I was invited to contribute flash fiction for an anthology devoted to the future of Anthropogenic Global Warming (AGW). Because I am highly skeptical of that explanation for alleged climate change, I submitted the following flash fiction. I was surprised that it was accepted.]

<u>Carbon Zero</u>

I don't know why I am writing this, or to whom. There are only a few survivors left here in our subterranean redoubt in the Peruvian Andes, and we all give thanks to the foresightedness of Mike Manx, eccentric billionaire and our unlikely savior.

Manx, always rebellious, made his first fortune by playing odds against that early 21st century pseudoscientific version of the medieval "dancing sickness," (whereby for unknown reasons, normal people take up destructive fads and practices, cult-like, without rational thought): "global warming," they called it.

Manx bought thousands of defunct wind turbines – those abandoned after the 2030s when petroleum engines became 99.5% efficient, and compact nuclear reactors appeared on every corner – for pennies on the dollar, converting his "aerial Cuisinarts" into the coolest of high-rise housing for the *uber*-rich.

Then, of course, the Sun had a severe Minimum; simultaneously the world's volcanoes began spewing out gigatons of the Earth's toxic inner gases, sun-blocking the thickened atmosphere, and all the glaciers returned with a vengeance.

Manx knew the Andes would be the safest place, but instruments now show all exits are blocked, under a kilometer of ice.

It's ironic, but our "carbon footprint" is now zero.

[*Author's Comments: This story originated when I read in Shelby Foote's Civil War books about the depredations carried out during piratical Union raids led by General Nathaniel P. Banks against non-combatants in northern Louisiana for the purpose of seizing Southern cotton, and the profitable bounty that it earned him.*]

<u>*War, With Incident*</u>

Vast forest shadows stretched ominously over the small clearing where Aunt Lizzie's ancient log cabin squatted in her scrubby cotton patch. 'Long about sundown, like a dark front of storm clouds, the Civil War rolled over us.

Through the walls of her cabin, an increasingly loud roar of cannons and shrieks assaulted our ears. But Aunt Lizzie had other priorities: "You finish yore supper," she said as the walls shook from a nearby explosion. Her ancient face so weathered you could never tell she had once been a Priestess in a far-away land, or so she claimed, she squinched up her eyes again. "Cain't do nothin' 'bout what's happenin' out there."

But it was hard for me, a twelve-year-old, to eat his grits and greens and drink his persimmon juice, knowing that grown men were killing each other out there in the woods. "Besides, get near a winder, yore gonna git a bullet in the head." I knew what Yankee bullets could do, saw it when they shot my parents and burnt our house, over in Louisiana. "Banks' Gorillas" they called themselves. I couldn't think of a Christian thing to call them; I just wanted them dead. But if Aunt Lizzie hadn't of found me the day before, wandering north without food, I would have been buzzard meat. So I listened to her.

"We'uns is stayin' out of this war. We got a bigger one goin' on." I never understood why the War for Southron Independence wasn't *our* war. But since I came into her care the day before, all she did was go on about some kind of ancient conflict with critters she called *ban-shees*, *afrits*, and *djinn.*

"Them *Others* is the real enemies, of ever' kind o' human bein'," she was saying. "They're–"

Ka-whoom! The wall behind her blew up, throwing me into a heap of furniture, with logs and chairs and food and utensils falling hither and yon. I was deafened, and in the awful silence that followed, I dug myself out of the rubble, eyes stinging. To my horror, I couldn't find Aunt Lizzie! Through the swirling clouds of dust and smoke, I could see where the chair she'd been sitting in was just broken sticks, her ample tote-sack dress now a crumpled bloody rag, like she'd vanished along with the wall behind her, along with my hearing.

Though totally deafened by the shell, my vision through the missing wall was unimpaired. There in the shadows across the patch, dozens of raggedy scarecrow-thin Confederates reeled under a wave of blue-uniformed soldiers. One of the Yankee attackers, a swashbuckler astride a coal-dark horse, saw me and galloped my way, raising his bloody saber. Behind this oncoming blue behemoth, part of my mind watched as the Southron soldiers melted into the woods, while the victorious bluecoats set fire to the trampled-down ruins of the cotton field.   Suddenly I knew these were the same gorillas who killed my folks.

With that realization, I was no longer afraid, just filled with rage. Unable to avoid my certain destruction, I picked up a four-foot-long piece of sharp, burning timber from the ruins. I was going to hit this Yankee devil if it was the last thing I did. I surely expected it would be.

In the midst of this silent chaos, a bright light blossomed behind me. When I turned, Aunt Lizzie – at least, what had been Aunt Lizzie, for now she was a young woman, clad in glistening bronze chest armor, holding a gigantic red spear – sat astride some kind of critter I had never seen, something all green scales and red claws and big white razor-sharp teeth, taking up nearly the whole room. And I swear, inside that ruined cabin, Aunt Lizzie *glowed!* She nodded and smiled. With her eyes and a twitch of her head, she indicated the approaching enemy, ten yards away.   Without thinking, I turned and threw my pitiful weapon with all my might.

As if shot from a cannon, my burning timber missile pierced the Yankee horseman, plunging right through his heart. In shock, I watched as he calmly brought his horse to a stop, put his saber back into its sheath, dismounted, and felt around his ruined chest.   As he pulled out the burning shaft and casually tossed it aside, I peed my pants. *What kind of devil* was *this?*

Instantly, Aunt Lizzie went into action on that great

beast of hers, charging directly at that Yankee officer with a glowing spear twenty feet long. Then, I swear, that bluecoat devil turned pure green and grew bulging fireball eyes as big as dinner plates, and tried to pull his sword back out of its scabbard. But it was too late; Aunt Lizzie had lanced him dead on and he sort of curled up into a green ball and vanished in a putrid puff of evil-smelling smoke. Aunt Lizzie dismounted and set her beast loose on the paralyzed, horrified Yankee soldiers in the field. I'd just as soon not remember that part.

Trembling, I ran over into the arms of Aunt Lizzie, who once more was a warm and familiar old lady in old rags, once more my savior. But now she had a perfumey odor about her, like lilacs and lavender.

"What did you *do,* Aunt Lizzie?" I asked, when I finally found my voice. "*Who* was that man, and *what* was that critter you rode, and *how* did you get to be so young and pretty?"

"Hush, young 'un. There's all kind of things you will learn when you get growed up. Just remember, there's a whole lot to learn, so you get yourself to a school just as soon as this war's over." The next day she packed me up a bag of food and kissed me and sent me off up in the direction of Little Rock, where some cousins lived.

I never went back, and I never learned what she meant about that *Other War.*

[PC speech – which I often refer to in my stories as 'Preferred Consensus' – continues to plague free societies. It may even be suicidal.]

<u>Foundation and Zombies</u>

"*Time travelers* brought us to our present situation," Senator Aciedo said loudly, trying to have his voice heard over the muffled roar of screams, grunts and groans echoing through the Capitol building from outside its thick walls. He paused as the *chump!-chump!-chump!* of AZ -47 decapitation rounds from the Capitol Guard guns grumbled loudly, then diminished.

The cacophony of screams, grunts and groans likewise now attenuated, he began again. "The Russians, damn their non-existent souls, should have known better than to mess with Father Time. *Chronos Unleashed*, indeed! If they had checked with us, the world wouldn't be having this – this –" Here he stumbled, searching for the proper word. *Cannot use the Z-word, absolutely cannot! The media would murder me!* "– this *apocalypse!*"

"Objection! Objection!" From the floor, the Opposition was screaming. Finally, one Senator was given the floor. "There is no evidence of any, any so-called *apocalypse,* for want of a better word. These *unfortunates* outside our chamber –" Aciedo grimaced as yet another crescendo of screams, grunts and groans steady built up "– are the victims of disease, of neglect, of ignorance. We should be working here to fund research to help them, not to –"

A sudden surge of raucous noise cut off the speaker, followed by a gagging odor of putrefaction. The Senate chamber doors creaked and groaned and finally burst inward from the brute force of wave after wave of pale-skinned, ragged and bloody figures, screaming, grunting, groaning, grasping at the Senators and their aides, biting them when they were able. Senator Aciedo recognized several Capitol guards among the rotting, stiff-legged invaders. *Damn! That virus acts fast!* he thought without thinking as he strapped on a respirator mask and unstrapped his own AZ-47, quickly mowing down the nearest group of gruesome attackers. He was gratified to see that all the Senate aides and other Senators were likewise firing their decap rounds, resulting in emaciated heads rolling this way and that like lawn bowling balls, green blood gushing the aisles, staining seats and TV monitors alike. *This stench alone is almost enough to kill you!* he thought. But death was only the beginning if this virus infected you!

Within five minutes, the Senate was once again back to normal, the hazmat-suited, ax-wielding Capitol Maintenance crew rapidly cleaning up the bulk of the mess with their usual aplomb, spraying disinfectants and deodorizers to wash away the stench of the decaying, decapitated bodies. And finishing the job on the few animated but immobile corpses left with heads attached.

Wiping green stains from his face mask before removing it, Senator Aciedo took the podium once more, and continued the day's business. "Our first witness will be Dr. Mesach Maximov, distinguished professor of science, formerly of the former nation of Russia. Dr. Maximov, if you please."

Maximov moved his massive Levantine frame into the chair behind the witness table. "When we Russians invented time travel, or *Vremya Zemalya*," he said, "we were very aware to prevent paradoxes. We could not change past, we would not interfere with the history, much as we would have liked." Senator Aciedo wondered just what kinds of changes the Russian would have liked to make – strangle Stalin in the crib, maybe? Or maybe Gorbachev?

"And so, we experimented with sending only immaterial, er, *materials*, into past and future. That is, we could send *minds* of time travelers back into past, into minds of past people, to observe, to remember, but not to affect actions of people of the past or future. And it worked! Was beautiful! The reports from St. Petersburg and October Revolution alone were –"

"Dr. Maximov," Senator Aciedo interrupted, "Thank you for your testimony. We are all aware of discovering that Ulanov was not quite the heroic figure some once made him out to be. But," his voice grew serious, "we are here to discuss the, uh, um, present situation, the virus that is affecting large numbers of our –"

"Objection! Objection!" the same Opposition voices interrupted. "The Senator is exaggerating the threat. He must stop these unfounded allegations!" Dozens of other Opposition Senators joined in, and Aciedo spread his hands in surrender.

"Enough, gentlemen," he moaned, "call it what you will. But I think the threat that we face must be described before it can be attended to. Dr. Maximov, would you address the, uh, present situation, and how time travel may have caused it?"

"*Da*," Maximov grimaced, his nose wrinkling at the residual smells left after Capitol Maintenance had finished their work. "As you know, Russian economy flourished when we were able to offer *Vremya Zemalya* over the Internet, allowing paying tourists to choose any time and place of their wishes. Projecting their minds by the millions, into watching surprises of the Pyramids, shock of Crucifixion, excitement of Coliseum Games, actual Atlantis, and –"

Aciedo banged his gavel. "Doctor, please, the *present situation*?"

"*Da*," the aging scientist said. "After one year of VZ, hundreds of millions of persons had paid milliards o f *yuan* for their VZ mind-traveling. Especially in Russia; almost every one of our citizens had escaped into golden past, a place of their choosing. Everyone but us – you, me and a few older scientists whose brains were just too old, too ossified, to accept VZ transfer protocols.

"And after one year, first reports began to come in. Human bodies, mindless, rotting, rampaging throughout our country. Emergency systems overcome. Few heroic medical doctors were able to strap down and investigate poor creatures. They found that bodies were infected with unknown virus. Strangely, brains of these creatures were operating only minimally, as if no consciousness present. And even minimal maintenance, involuntary systems, had shut down, so bodies were self-degenerating."

"Unknown virus seems to be initiated upon the return of VZ'ers. Triggering mechanism must be at quantum level, because we were unable to view even with our electron microscopes. And then outbreaks in your own country began." The scientist shook his head, shuddering.

"Yes, Dr. Maximov," Senator Aciedo took over, "we are familiar with that outbreak, quite familiar." Aciedo could not bring himself to violate the Preferred Consensus, could not say the Z-word. *Unfortunates* was necessary, but not at all sufficient to describe the literally lost souls of the VZ'ers. But just as unfortunate were their victims, when a VZ'er's bite – saliva – could instantly infect and override a healthy person's immune system. "But how," he continued, "did this happen?"

The Russian sighed and groaned. "Minds of VZ travelers, those who traveled many, many times, somehow got stuck in past. Some kind of accommodation to minds that left our present too many times. Maybe each trip took away little consciousness, allowed little more ability to stay in past host? My colleagues in former Russia were believing that as mind diminished, normal viruses in body reacted to conquer remaining intelligence. Whole body became virus machine."

Grimacing, Senator Aciedo said, "You mean, every one of the, uh, *unfortunates* is driven by a virus, their minds totally gone?" He took a deep breath, "And just where are these lost minds? Do you know?"

Maximov gave a Russian shrug of hopelessness. "VZ'ers are *all* virus. Bodies rot because virus is not alive, has no reason to maintain anything but attack mode in order to propagate. No other purpose.

"As for minds of more than billion people, VZ'ers, we think they are marooned somewhere in past. Nothing can be done for them. No rescue. No bodies to return to."

Aciedo silently thanked God that he himself had been too old for online time-traveling. He had viewed the rather shocking re-creations of momentous past events based on descriptions of the VZ'ers who, in the early months of the craze, had returned with fantastic stories of high technologies, lost civilizations, and reports of religious and historical events that differed wildly from accepted versions. *Truth hurts*, he recalled a Russian saying. *Indeed!*

A thought struck the Senator and he blurted out, "Dr. Maximov, if all of these hundreds of millions of people, billions maybe, are stuck in the minds of people in the past, can they have any effect on our past? Is our past really our own?"

The Russian put his large hands over his bearded face. "As virus degeneration progressed, some VZ returnees told stories of physical interaction with hosts in past. They said they could make hosts do things. We feared for integrity of past. Afraid of making changes we could not control or predict. Some returnees said they had been active in the bodies of Napoleon, Akhenaton, King George Three, some American Presidents, some Arabs, many Roman Emperors, even Biblical prophets. But before we could discover cause and effect, virus plague occurred, and you know rest."

Aciedo spread his hands. "Then billions of people are in the past, changing it as we speak, with the knowledge of modern history and technology. What have you done?"

Before the scientist could answer, Aciedo's attention was grabbed by the sounds of yet another onrush of screaming, grunting, groaning mobs of VZ'ers. This time, however, they charged through in numbers that overwhelmed the remaining Capitol Guards. In the mad crush that followed, one of the creatures bit the Senator through his sleeve, taking away a chunk of suit and skin. The gusher of Aciedo's arterial blood immediately attracted other undead, and they converged on the Senator.

Aciedo had only seconds of consciousness left before the virus took control. In the dark descent toward oblivion, he wondered why his final thoughts were of Ambrose Bierce.

[Author's Comments: Expeditions to the seafloor at Antikythera, Greece, are continuing.   Who knows what treasures lie in wait?]

<u>*Wreck Support*</u>

(The following mysterious message was translated from a form of Ancient Greek found on a scroll on a sealed amphora taken from a sunken craft in the vicinity of the Greek island of Antikythera, where underwater explorers in the early 20th Century had found a geared, computer-like mechanism on the ocean floor. The esoteric meanings in the text are unknown, and made public here for the first time in hopes of stimulating research into the apparent rites and religious paraphernalia referred to in the ancient message.)

```
From:  AoM, TG
```

```
Subject:   Teknikos Support for a
non-working komputoros
```

I am returning the attached piece of worthless donkey dung machinery that you inaccurately called a "*komputoros digitos*". I was assured by your sales *hoi* that the Zeus-cursed device would assist me in my start-up invasion business plans. It has most certainly not performed as advertised.

Right out of its packing amphora, the device

malfunctioned. When I went looking for the abrasive tool accessory supposed to be included, in order to smooth the intricate gearing sufficiently to mesh properly, the arrow signal indicators pointed to the inscription "File Not Found."

Trying to use my fingers, my "digits" to turn the disks as illustrated on the amphora, I found that the so-called *"systemos operatos"* could not operate the hardware – the gears and wheels – I nearly broke my royal ring fingers! And the so-called "software", the papyrus texts, looked like Greek to me, a proud Macedonian.

When I tried to program the device to calculate odds on events in the upcoming Olympic Games, an opportunity to provide much-needed funds for my business plan, the arrow signals pointed to "insufficient memory", an insult to my carefully memorized gear placements. Moronic toothed wheels! Whoever believed that dumb disks could compete with Aristocratic Intelligence?

I was thus unable to calculate the proper phases of Artemis and her tides, which were of utmost importance to my business plan. My spread sheets of papyrus documentation remain blank without this information. It is imperative that I receive a working machine by return vessel. My planned expedition to the legendary New World, far beyond the Pillars of Hercules, depends upon it!

If the requested *technikos* support and a replacement *komputoros* are not promptly received, I shall sail to your city, slaughter all the men, enslave your women and children, watch your temples crash

and burn, and wipe all memory of your existence.
Have a nice *hemera*,

Alexandros of Macedonia,
AKA, "The Great"

[Author's Comments: I have always felt that in the future we may see matter transmitters.   As happened with ham radio operators and then the plethora of computer and software "hackers", we will probably also experience amateur *matter transmitters.]*

<u>...*Plus C'est La Même Chose,*</u>
<u>*Or,*</u>
<u>*Maps, Live!*</u>

"We are gathered here for an historic occasion," the blond announcer whispered knowingly, intoning a profundity that his bleached appearance belied, "the first contest of the world's amateur matter transmitter operators.   They will attempt to 'matter-mit' – or 'chop', in their vernacular – the most complex structures that their machines can achieve. The object judged to be the most complex, most original, arriving here in New World Orders in Brussels, will determine the winner of this test of the amateur competitors."

Blondie then called up stock videos of the earlier matter-mitting machines of Hieronymous, Bigelow, Gallimore, and the other pioneers who had developed the near-magical devices that now powered most manufacturing economies in the mid-21st Century. The 3D TV showed the usual hilarious outtakes from early serious experiments that went awry – golf balls embedded in stones, beer cans morphed into Klein bottles through weird 4D transmission errors, left-handed sculptures made dexter by faulty 'mitters.

Blondie's narration did not follow some of the matter-mitter trials that resulted in grotesque death and dismemberment, though those were easily accessible on any of the competing World Webs. And mentioned none of the game-changing military applications, those that had made the world safer from terrorists than ever before. Even the Pentagonal Building wouldn't say where those terrorists had gone when involuntarily matter-mitted by Special Forces teams. That nebulous revelation had been fearsome enough to overcome almost all fanatical fervor for a couple of decades now. And had effectively ended all attempts to matter-mit living organisms. "You can't chop meat!" the saying went.

Blondie's next segment featured Weird Hal, the world's best-known (if most notorious) "chopper". In years past, the extremely obese amateur matter-mitter had been caught sending real fossils to the Moon and Mars, there for the CHindi walker-bots to pick up, causing either momentary panic or elation among spacenuts and scientificos. But amateur matter-mitting was still in its infancy, with most choppers content to send and receive trivial toys and trinkets, as their grandcestors had exchanged DX cards.

At the moment, on all competing World Webs, Weird Hal was happily singing at his chopping console: "My daddy was a hacker/My Grandpa was a ham/When it comes to choppin' matter/I'm the best there am, by damn!" Off-key and off-base, his voice grated like the stripped gears of an ancient machine tool.

"Our probability AI's give Weird Hal the edge

today," the announcer continued as Hal's grating voice and grossly overweight image faded. "As probably the world's most successful 'chopper', we eagerly anticipate what surprises he may have in store.

"But today" – a pregnant pause – "Hal is also up against newcomer choppers from the U.K., the PRC and the USA." Scenes flashed on and off, spiraling in, fading in and out, a maelstrom of unknown competitors from undistinguished or faded nations: Unified Korea, Patriotically Reconstituted Chinas, and the Union of Socialist Americas. Video closeups showed Hal surrounded by his quoit-shaped chopping console, the man-mountain guzzling one beer after another, singing verse after ever more obscene verse of his Chopper's Anthem. With his massive frame blocking the camera view, Hal quickly opened a shoebox-sized device, shoving his entry into the transmitting chamber, ready to chop.

"And now the final entries," Blondie said. The scene shifted to a one meter nano-crystalline cube on a small table. "Each contestant is required to matter-mit their entry into this receiver. Instruments will determine the safety of the object; then the judges can dissolve the cube to inspect each entry closely.

"And now we begin. Entry one, from Shakaville, Sudafrica." The crystal cube clouded with swirling clouds, colorful mini-storms, finally clearing to reveal a dark, contoured object about half a meter square. The cube wisped away and the four judges held up a delicately carved artifact. "And the entry is a ceremonial tribal mask." The announcer was less than enthusiastic.

For nearly an hour, entry after entry materialized inside the receiving cube: a miniature da Vinci sculpture from New Rome, an intricate series of *matroshka* dolls from Novaya Moskva, and more, but nothing truly spectacular. For that, the world waited on its weird anti-hero.

"All eyes are now on Hal," the announcer said breathlessly, as the famous chopper ostentatiously typed his transmission sequence on an ancient touchscreen.

"But, wait, I am told that an unauthorized matter-mitter is attempting to send in something." On the screen, the receiving cube seemed to *burp*. Blondie's voice was almost a scream: "Someone is trying to upstage the world's most famous chopper!"

Billions of viewers stared as the crystal cube seemed to experience a mini-war inside itself: boiling, roiling luminescent clouds appeared, then vanished; chaos fighting chaos. "Who could be interfering with Weird Hal this way? What's happening?"

Suddenly the cube cleared, revealing a small rectangular block-like object in the chamber. Just inches in each dimension, tiny in comparison to the previous entries, it was predominantly blue and gold, with bold yellow lettering. One of the judges gave a hand signal and the receiving cube vanished. Quickly all the judges surrounded the receiver, handling the strange object. They called for an assistant, who shortly returned and handed one a small metal device. Within minutes, the judges began laughing and nodding.

One judge held up a metal can, now opened,

showing pinkish material inside. "We have a winner," the judge said with a nervous smile. "Not only was our so-far anonymous victor able to override Hal, but sent us a metal can containing animal tissue and other materials – a double victory, of both complexity and originality.

"This unexpected, unauthorized entry represents the next stage in amateur matter-mitting." He shook his head, the smile gone. "It was inevitable, of course."

As the camera zoomed in closer, Blondie read the yellow lettering on the exterior of the gold-topped, rectangular can.

Puzzled, he said, "It reads – *Spam*."

[Author's Comments: The U.S. Department of Homeland Security asked SIGMA members to speculate on threats to our Transportation Security over the next 25 years, and to suggest appropriate defenses.   This was my contribution.]

Pilots of the Purple Twilight

Standing on the modest tourist platform atop the Great Pyramid, Jawar Al-Shalani watched as the Giza Disney monorail from Cairo International Airport unloaded its passengers at the base, some 200 meters below. He smiled as they disembarked from the sleek, air-conditioned bullet cars into the blazing summer sun and walked to the open escalator that would bring them up to him. He thought, *Even the Disney franchisee couldn't persuade the Supreme Council of Antiquities to allow cool comfort to those ascending this forbidding slope.*

He turned his attention to his guests as two dozen investors and *Omedian reporters* (with their ever-present bulbous recording headgear, he noted) arrived, greeting each one in turn, escorting the obvious acrophobes to the crowded center of the platform, leaving the more adventurous leaning against the transparent walls. As the complaints and murmurs died down, Al-Shalani began what he hoped would be his final pitch for financial support.

"All of you, my friends, my associates, my confidants, you from the Omedia," he said, "let me direct your attention to the H-2 aerocraft behind me." As if their attention hadn't been focused on his brainchild since before their train arrived at the Pyramid. Attached to a shimmering, nearly-transparent five-meter wide walkway extending out a hundred meters from this very tip of this ancient monument, floated a gigantic silver cylinder, its ends capped by hemispheres, glistening in the Egyptian sun. "The H-2," he said proudly, "is seventy-five meters in diameter and four hundred meters in length. It has a bulk cargo carrying capacity of three thousand metric tons, not including the crew of three."

Behind him, the enormous whale-like craft moved slowly, side to side, as if in response to its master's voice. "Your OmnIpad displates will show you the details. H-2 is shaped like the Zeppelins of old, but her technologies are new and still developing. Her lifting capability comes from the evacuated aerogel that forms her lifting configuration. Coated with layers of thin nanodiamond shell, she is invulnerable to anything short of nanukes. Morphable thrusters direct air flow to stabilize her attitude, as is happening here, where the hot winds rise. To finish with details, the crew compartment is atop the ship, her cargo bays are below. Detachable, of course, in case of challenge. To be dropped at sea, if necessary, and harmlessly recovered there."

He smiled at that. Any cargo craft approaching Europe or North America or East Asia today either had detachable cargo bays or risked immediate nanuke shootdown. All the big boys – America, the Four Chinas, Japan, Europe – had learned their lessons very well since NutJob's Guards had hurt them so badly twelve years before with simultaneous air and sea EMP attacks. They wouldn't be hit *that way* again. And not by that nation – NutJob and his country no longer existed.

"And what are the first markets for our new carrier?" anxiously asked one of Al-Shalani's investors, a banker from First Baghdad Ecominium, "America, Four Chinas, where? Will the Big Boys even let us in? Let us land?"

"That big bag of gel can't travel very fast, either," another chimed in. "The cost of time in transit will be too great." Other nervous comments erupted, giving Al-Shalani another opportunity to brag about his achievement.

"Since NutJob's attacks," he continued, "the Big Boys no longer allow any highspeed air transport into their nations, as you know. For example, United North America has a standing policy that any high-speed aircraft, identified or not, approaching its two hundred kilometer limit, will be immobilized or blogged by their directed energy defense systems." Indeed, last week's OmNews carried the stories of how the UNA BLOG (the Beason Longrange Omnidirectional Grazer) had dispatched a large group of Brazilian tourists whose aircraft somehow strayed northward while attempting to visit Free Havana.

"At only one hundred kilometers per hour, we are no threat to anyone, and they know it. On our first test flight last week, from Gaza International to Wilmington, we were slow enough that the mini-UAVs of the UNA Central Authority for Security of the

Americas, CASA, were able to orbit and surveil us to their heart's content, spray us with many layers of nanosensors, and even deposit their sensor payloads to the cargo and crew compartments as we leisurely approached their shores.

"Needless to say, this open and trustworthy approach minimizes our inspection fees, tariffs, and quarantine period. Our international competitors, using slow and large reciprocating engine aircraft, cannot compete with our size, our capacity and our speed. We can fabricate H-2s of any size, theoretically, and could totally automate them – no pilot, no crew – if ever allowed to by the Big Boys.

"And because we require each of our shippers to utilize our proprietary H-2 nanogel encapsulating system, every single shipment is characterized and/or sterilized. Our manifest is sent directly to UNA and the others; we know of no way to hack this system." Along the side of the H-2, the iconic logo for his company blinked on, glowing: the silhouette of the Great Pyramid with the H-2 tethered to it. "This is the future of safe, secure international transport."

"And why is it called H-2, Dr. Al-Shalani?" an Omedian, this one a female reporter for the *Kabul Times*, asked. "Is it filled with hydrogen? And dangerous, like the, the, uh, Hindenberg?"

Al-Shalani smiled, "The name is indeed an homage to those hydrogen-filled flying deathtraps of old. But as I have said, ours is very fine aerogel in a vacuum. The name is from English: AITCH-TWO, or Aerogel International Transport Cargo Handlers – The World Over."

His audience mollified for the moment, Al-Shalani, waved a hand. The transparent walkway opaqued, and a crewperson beckoned them all to come aboard.

[Author's Comments: The story is self-explanatory. And it does mention the collapse of the European Union, which may be in the process of occurring now, in mid-2016.]

What Engineers Know

Dr. Grandiveer Plone, renowned physicist, accepted the Nobel Prize of 2012 in his field with great humility and dignity, acknowledging his debt to his university, his research institute, his graduate students, "And a lone United States Army field engineer whom I met during the late unpleasantness in Arabia Felix."   Mutters washed over the mostly Scandinavian audience; they had given Dr. Plone his award in spite of his service as a Special Ops colonel in the American military, those historic but warlike accomplishments not rising in their minds to his later achievement in theoretical physics.

Oblivious to – or perhaps enjoying – the discomfort of his hosts, Dr. Plone went on, "It was right before the restoration of the Mecca Crater that I met Doc Briggs, the compleat engineer. He was one man who could design anything, build anything, repair anything – the most accomplished human being I have ever met." Sgt. Briggs' exploits in the Mideast Wars were all too well known to the still simmering Swedes, and to the millions of unwelcome refugees who had fled the collapse of the old E.U.   Mercenaries like Briggs, though necessary, were still evils.   Even when their paychecks came from the new Scandinavian Union.

"Doc Briggs and I had just got ourselves stuck in a sand dune a few dozen klicks outside Mecca, when the Kaaba Bomb went off, a ground blast of only a few kilotons. Fortunately we were shielded by the dune, but our HumVee was rolled over until it was a literal wreck…" The hubbub of the crowd was rising now, and Plone acknowledged the audience's indignation. "I say to you, my fellow Laureates, researchers and hosts, this war story directly relates to my discovery. I beg your indulgence." The vast hall became quieter, puzzlement replacing anger on the upturned faces.

"Long story short," the physicist continued, "Briggs was able to throw that vehicle back together with great skill and some other basic ingredients, which enabled us to get back on the road and …" He didn't have to fill in that blank; the whole world knew how that particular trip had ended, how he and Sgt. Briggs had brought about the end of the war. *I'm sure Doc Briggs will have something to say about that*, Plone thought.

"A year later, I picked up my research at New Mexico State University, where I had left it for my two years active service in the Reserves. And something Doc Briggs had said that day near Mecca stuck in my mind, a phrase I just couldn't forget. The fact that he essentially rebuilt that famous HumVee from nothing was just too outstanding a memory.

"From my Weblog publications since, you all understand how, up until my return, I had been stymied in my investigation of superstring theory. Then with Doc Briggs' inspiration, I was able to make the imaginative leap, and that of course led to all of the practical new 2D-ultrathread applications that now form the basis of all our electrogravitomagnetic industries."

The applause began timidly, caught on a bit, and reached a level of Scandinavian politeness, then declined. But Plone was not through, not this day. "During the project, utilizing the White Sands–Cobblestone N-dimensional nanoreactor, I discovered that superstrings were actually tubular in shape. With the Briggs model in mind, I was able to open up a superstring and lay it out flat, giving rise to the term, 'two-dimensional ultrathreads'.

"Further tests showed that the superstring tubes are the primary mechanism by which all gravitrons and chronons are transported, ducted instantaneously – or faster – all over the Universe. They provide the basic underlying structure of the Universe, and my theories show that there are no further sub-components. Opening these ducts gave us access to incredible amounts of free energy, paradox-free time travel, and the other two truly important surprises that we all appreciate so much in our daily lives."

Plone paused. From his right, Doc Briggs emerged from behind thick blue curtains. Beaming broadly, the short, muscular, graying man, bedecked in tuxedo, strode across the stage to take Plone's hand. "Never saw 'em give the Peace Prize here in Stockholm, Grandy," he muttered through his thick beard, "but we'll take 'em both won't we? And you getting another one of 'em in physics, too. Ain't life a bitch?"

"Amen, Elon," Plone whispered back. "Ladies and gentlemen and alternate genders," he said aloud, "let me introduce Doctor Elon Briggs, who helped me save the world that day in Arabia, and who opened the doors to the Universe as well." Applause was still hesitant, but a little more than polite, though reluctant.

"Elon told me something, that day five years ago in Arabia Felix, a profound truth. When I discovered, working from his cue, that superstrings are indeed ducts, and that when opened and laid out, they are flat, 2D ultrathreads, tape-like structures, I realized that he and all those other engineers were absolutely correct.

"Truly, the Universe *is* held together with 'duct tape'!"

[I wrote the first version of this story in the early 1980s, for a contest looking at engineering in the Year 2020. Some of the concepts later formed the basis of a NASDAQ-listed Virtual Reality company I co-founded in the 1990s (Muse Technologies, Inc.), and the "consens" business model is now a normal mode of operation in the Internet Age.]

<u>2020: The Chimera Engineer</u>

The kimmie interrupted my programmed dream just as the bad guys rode over the hill, six-guns a-blazing. *Never fails,* I thought as I woke up, *but work is work.* "Logon, fuzzball," I whispered as the little hairy brown bracelet-of-artificial-life that lives on my wrist extended its tendrils and made modem contact with the neural-link computer system. *I'll never know why I designed that thing to mew,* I groaned, yawning.

In an instant, the other Freepartners of Consensual Enterprises came on line via neural-link: Kathay, the InGeneEer, from *Novaya Moskva*, Copernicus; M'Ngo, kimmie packaging specialist, Pretoria-Shakaville; and the usual ten or twelve others from around the Near System. No Asteroiders this time; *must be harvest time out there,* I mused.

We exchanged traditional greetings before Atilla popped into our heads. "Farside IV has proposed a contract for three thousand personal meditative interfacers. The profit potential is satisfactory. I had hoped for greater response," he/she said dourly. (Atilla

– a real slave driver – is our neural-link computer system. I don't know what the acronym stands for, but it's appropriate: in finding and negotiating contracts for our Freepartners, he/she wheels and deals extremely aggressively.   Although we all designed his/her characteristics, he/she does put us all through our paces. One day, I'd like to reprogram him/her for more courtesy, but I sometimes think he/she wouldn't allow it.)

"But it does appear that we have a minimum design capability on line."   (I don't know which one of us programmed Atilla's sarcasm.)   "The specs are the usual." They appeared, floating in space, right at arm's length. (Atilla's bag of tricks includes space animation, remember.) *Right, the usual,* I thought, *too much work for too little money.* I said nothing. Atilla only senses gross emotion, so my ersatz disgust didn't register as a negative vote.

"Three days!" M'Ngo objected, as did a few others. "Lunar Transport, Ltd., take three days for delivery! We'll miss the deadline. You've screwed up this time, you dumb system!" Atilla calmly (and patiently too, I noticed) explained that Nippon Orbital had a module standing by to fabricate the design once we were finished. By using a small LT, Ltd., electromagnetic launcher that would become available in six hours, Farside delivery could be accomplished in under the three days – and we could collect a good bonus. I whistled softly at my projected share.

Nineteen whistles later, a quorum of Freepartners had agreed to do the job. A few went back to sleep or whatever – lucky them, with plush credit balances. The rest of us, we went to work.

I gave the neural commands that enabled the workspace program to commence. Those Freepartners on my physical design subgroup linkage saw what I saw: Atilla's realtime animation program would generate three-dimensional images for us to manipulate, floating right in front of us. We could enlarge, reduce, even microscopically inspect the design; we could run tests on the computer model to simulate exactly the real thing – change materials, modify environmental factors, do destructive testing – anything we could visualize, and do some things (like with magnetic and paraphysical fields) that only Atilla could sense. The circuit/genesplicers would likewise do their tricks and we would package the results into the human-factored, optimized container system – carbon, silicon, or kimmie.

Using Atilla's slowmode display, my subgroup reviewed our last few hundred designs in minute detail, elapsed time: 90 seconds. Atilla's consensual sensors collected our responses and showed us what we liked best – an early model meditative interfacer design, crustacean shell, crystal molded in a .01G cylindrical gravity field. *Just right for Nippon Orbital's available facility*! I grinned.

With my submicro fingerpad transmitters, I space-sculpted a few minor modifications in one corner. (Atilla monitors the fingertip trajectories and animates in three dimensions whatever I "sculpt." That's one of my personal specialties. There are others.) M'Ngo and a new Freepartner threw in some dollops of infra-colors and we consensed – a nice design. Now if the

InGeneEers had done their part...

Kathay and her subgroup linked in with their kimmie design; Atilla said that we had a good match among physical and kimmie designs, and that manufacturability was nominal. We had it made! (That last, almost literally; Nippon Orbital's neural-link observer computer had picked up the development in progress and had sketched out anticipated requirements in parallel. Farside's personal meditative interfacers would be on the way to the Moon on the next LT, Ltd. launcher.)

We all congratulated each other and downlinked. As Atilla displayed my share of the day's profits, I was elated. My accounts were coming along fine; the investment program automatically took over a percentage of the new income, and my risk portfolio expanded to include some new protein mining ventures on Titan. Feeling generous, I reviewed my voluntary tithe-tax disbursement. I increased a portion of it to help the increasing numbers of unfortunates still struggling by in the pitiful remnants of old SovBloc Asia. Would they ever learn? (I deducted an equal amount from my contributions to the old Union of North America; they didn't have much to do anymore.)

My chemical kimmic flew across the room with my usual morning transfusion of vitamins, minerals and caffeine. Feeling drowsy before the concoction hit, I yawned again and opened the cleardome to view the great undersea craters here at *Los Condos del Cuba Perdida.*

[Author's Comments: Some conspiracies are serious, others merely atrocious...]

<u>***Rite of Privacy***</u>

The inn was dark, but I could see the fat man sweating, even in the mottled reflection of the old mirror behind the bar where we were silting. He said, "God, Gary, I don't know how to say this, but I think I'm onto the Secret Masters!"

I didn't respond; calmly I sipped my Scotch and watched Wallace's face collapse in disappointment at my nonreaction. "Gary, did you hear what I said?" His voice, more insistent now, rose in pitch and volume, and we were beginning to attract attention from other dark corners of the establishment, attention I didn't care to have. I put down the shot glass and put an index finger to my lips. Wallace glared an instant and dropped his voice to a whisper.

"It started when I got that do-it-yourself kit for a backyard satellite dish." I chuckled, trying to imagine my ten-thumbed insurance salesman friend assembling something as intricate as a satellite receiving station. In all our college years, a decade ago, he had barely been able to place a long-play album on a record player. He didn't notice my amusement. "Took me three months altogether" – verified my hunch, I thought – "and like to never have got it to work. None of the diagnostics panned out, not a damned channel came in that was supposed to, and my old lady was getting really pissed at the money spent for nothing." Had to give him credit, Wallace was persistent; don't know that even I could function with that large trollish wife of his bitching over my shoulder.

"Decoder EPROM turned out to be the problem." I was impressed; most people don't even know about Erasable Programmable Read-Only Memory chip technology that is at the heart of the satellite decoding system. I suspected my old college friend had acquired quite a bit of knowledge in the years since I'd seen him last. He'd always operated at genius level, and I had often wondered why he'd gone into Business instead of staying in Engineering, my own career route. Maybe for money? My database search had shown that he was worth a ton of money, even before his satellite dish project.

"Tell me more," I said, motioning to the barkeep for another round of doubles. Wallace was talking and I wanted to hear more. Everything. "What next?"

Wallace must have picked up on the tone of my voice. His eyes jerked left and right, trying to find bad guys in the dark. I smiled and shook my head. "Just me, Wallace. I'm the only spook here. Go on, what happened?"

"I decided to re-program an EPROM myself, on my home personal computer. I hooked up an ultraviolet 'PROM burner' from Audio Shack and played around with various coding techniques." At my obvious reaction, it was his time to smile. "Simple, Gary, really it was. Hell, the Shack has manuals on how to do purt' near everything with decoders and crypto." I nodded. So that's how it had started, Wallace's dangerous road to ultimate wealth and power.

"Anyhow, kicked around the crypto codes I had used when I was a draftee in the National Security Agency and during my stint as a co-op programmer at Sandia National Laboratories. Used some old Developing Intelligence para-programs. Duck soup after that, old pal." Swallowing a full shot of straight Scotch, he tried to assume a stance of sophistication and fearlessness. It didn't work. His story did ring a bell, but the available bio database had skimmed over his year in the Army and his six months in New Mexico after that. It was all adding up.

"Whew, strong stuff, Gary," he commented, his voice a bit stronger now, whether from the lubrication or the influence of the alcohol I couldn't tell. I just nodded and continued to sip. Around the bar the faces in dark corners were paying us no mind. I was glad of that fact and hoped Wallace would keep his voice low

"I aimed the finished arrangement at the coordinates where the new NipStar satellite was supposed to be, cranked up the gain, and sat back to watch. Wanted to pick up some of those Oriental art films, the pornos, you know? Imagine my surprise when I started watching tomorrow's news!" I gulped and nearly choked on my drink. Wallace laughed.

He quickly filled me in on the fantastic channel he had been watching the last three months. One hundred-per-cent accurate prognostications of stock market trends, for example. Almost perfect predictions of elections, coups, and power grabs around the world. Even the outbreaks of strikes and wars! "Totally awesome, Gary. At first I thought it was some kind of religious program, you know, then maybe a science fiction story, like *The Time Machine,* you know?" I shook my head. Speculation was not in my line of business; engineering principles are immutable, so good engineers don't have opinions. *Just the facts, ma'am!*

"But it dawned on me that it wasn't the future I was watching, but some kind of secret power structure, here and now! The TV programs were slickly produced and featured some well-known personalities in all fields – politicians and bankers and military of all countries, lawyers, some academics, one or two well-known writers," – I whistled at the science fiction editor he mentioned; I wouldn't have believed it once – "and a bunch of other people I never heard of." I wasn't looking at him anymore, but stared straight across the bar into the mirror. Wallace caught my eyes in the reflections. "Hell, you know all of this. You got the tape I sent you, didn't you? That's why you're here, isn't it?"

I spoke slowly. "Wallace, old friend, the answers to your questions are yes and no." His mirror image frowned and lifted another full glass of booze and gulped it down. I turned and spoke directly to him, waiting a bit until he shook off the burning esophageal experience. "You believed what you saw didn't you, old friend?"

He nodded. "Hell, Gary, after a month of checking those predictions against newspapers, I decided I was onto something, so I cashed in." *Aptly put*, I thought. "You certainly did, Wallace. Rolled your hundred and fifty thousand in savings up to – what was it, seven million? Not bad for two months, was it?"

His mouth dropped open. "I never told you about that, how –?" He smiled. "Because you're CIA, right? Got access to everybody's files?"

"Yes and no, Wallace. You called me because you know I've been a CIA communications engineer since graduation. You wanted to know how much the CIA knew about your Secret Masters. Maybe protect you if you were attracting too much attention. Am I right?"

"That's about it, Gary. So you boys know all about the NipStar channel and the decoding and everything? Gonna sic the IRS on me?" I shook my head and sighed. He smiled and shrugged and pulled out a small plastic bag with a dark object inside it. "I'm completely clean. No insider trading, no SEC. Even the IRS can't touch me. I carry the chip with me at all times." Tapping the bag, he said, "Electrostatically protected so it won't be zapped and get its memory wiped out." I grimaced anew at that statement. Damn if he wasn't just too, too brilliant!

I motioned toward the darkness and four large but well-dressed goons came and surrounded my old friend. The barkeep pretended not to notice. Wallace protested, "Gary, you said you didn't care! The CIA didn't care! What's going on?"

"Wallace, old pal, the CIA and the IRS don't know and don't care, except for a very, very few. But 1 also have another job, working for some people who care very much." I pocketed the plastic bag with the EPROM chip and led the way out of the bar with a strangely quiet Wallace and the four goons following.

"Are they going to –?"

I shook my head. "You won't feel a thing, I

promise. And you'll be happier than you've ever known. I promise that too, Wallace. That's why I took this assignment. You are - you *were* - my friend. Good-bye."

"But – don't I even get to know what the charges are? Who the people behind this are? The Secret Masters of the World, is that it?" The goons were shoving him into a long black limo, and only his panicky face showed before the door shut.

"Close enough, Wallace. For you, entirely *too* close." The door slammed and the limo sped away into darkness. I sighed. There had been worse assignments, very much worse. But this time I had been told that Wallace would only suffer a partial mind wipe, much like a small induced stroke, losing only the memories of the last ten years or so. Otherwise no violence. My bosses let me have that small favor. I had also requested that his wife disappear both from his memory and from his life. *Compensation,* I thought. *It all evens out.*

My bosses are not unnecessarily cruel, or even ungrateful. I had been able to save my friend's life, but they insisted on absolute protection of their privacy. I mean, Hell, you can't let just *anybody* have unauthorized access to *Cabal TV!*

[Author's Comments: We don't have this kind of dentistry yet, but do note the "wrist computer"; some kinds of tech outstrip others. And my son, the dentist, says that the proper term would be "nanodontist"]

<u>A Visit to the Nanodentist</u>

"I hate dentists," Orly Williams said that morning to his wife. "The agony of the waiting, the anticipation of the pain of the drill, the terrible magazines in the lobby."

"How long has it been, dear?" Nadine asked. Orly sneered. *Easy for her to ask a stupid question,* he thought. *Her teeth are in perfect condition, while I suffer from chips, worn enamel, loose fittings, and a brand new cavity that a popcorn kernel located for me last night at the movie theater.*

"Fifteen years, dear. Why do you ask?" he said aloud. Surely she wasn't thinking that –?

"Since before the turn of the century? Time enough, my love. You are just behind the times. Dentistry doesn't even hurt at all anymore." She came closer, proudly pointing at each of her precisely aligned, perfectly proportioned, all white teeth. "See what a beautiful job Dr. Andrew Lutz did for me. Didn't hurt a bit. Inexpensive too.

"And they call it *nanodentistry* now, Orly."

Orly believed her about the name: he'd seen the holo ads for "NanoDent, the Ultimate Toothpaste", with all of the little molecular cartoon creatures cleaning teeth.   Orly *didn't* believe her about the pain.   He recalled his parents telling him the same thing some four decades back.   He also recalled the needle injections into his gums, the devilish whirring of the dentist's drill, the excruciating pain when an undeadened nerve reacted to the inquisitioner's probing instrument of torture.   No way would he ever do that again.   Maybe some of these newfangled plasto-teeth from the discount store would do the trick?

Nadine smiled sweetly at him, determined to bring the benefits of new technology to her husband.   "I knew you were old-fashioned, sweets, so 1 made the appointment for you, at Dr. Lutz's, tomorrow morning. You won't feel a thing."

Orly fainted.

"It's called *nanodentistry* now, Mr. Williams," the toothy, attractive dental assistant was saying as she led Orly, trembling and heartsick, into the dental chamber. "Nothing is the same as the old ways.   We have this fantastic new technology that does all of the work for the dentist.   Spray it into your mouth.   Gets down into your gums, your teeth, your bloodstream.   Does all of the repairs.   You won't feel a thing!'

Orly didn't believe her, so he climbed warily into the recliner and prayed to the gods of anesthetics that he would soon be out of this hell.   An old, old story about a sadistic family dentist kept echoing through his brain. He peered into every comer of the plush, cornerless room, just waiting for the little demons to approach him, to start carving out his teeth one by painful each.

Dr. Andrew Lutz was a tall, dark glad-hander,

reminiscent of an old-time politician, back a decade or two when people used to pay attention to that sort of thing, back before the worldwide teledemocracy revolution. "Mr. Williams, am 1 ever happy to see you." Orly hated him. "Did you know that you last visited a dentist back in –" the nanodentist paused, stroked an input strip on his left wrist computer, stared surprised at Orly "–in 1992? Sir, that must be some kind of record! You do know that we don't even call ourselves dentists anymore?"

"I know. *Nanodentists;"* Orly said with some sarcasm, his head feeling heavy as the electronic headrest soothed him. He felt a warmth emanating from around his neck, a susurrant comfort that soon spread over his body. He was totally relaxed.

By this time Dr. Lutz had opened Orly's mouth and was probing around inside with a pencil-sized flashing device, much like his own pocket laser. "My, my, Mr. Williams, we have been a bad boy," he said. He pointed the instrument at a blank wall and squeezed. A video appeared on the wall, close-ups of the dental wreck that Orly called his mouth.

"You've got symptoms of TMJ, gingivitis, malocclusions, bruxism, misalignment, chipped teeth, and several recent incidences of dental caries." Orly noted with grim satisfaction that he himself had diagnosed at least half of those without a dentist's – correction – *nanodentist's* – training. *My part was for free, too.*

Orly gulped. "What do – what do you – I mean, when –?"

"Dear, dear Mr. Williams;' Dr. Lutz laughed, at the

same time punching his right wrist computer terminal furiously, "all of these conditions, though quite rare in most of the world now, are easily handled!' He patted Orly on the head. "It will only take a few minutes for the nano-nation in my lab to turn out the older design of nanomechanisms that will recondition your poor teeth and gums.

"Now while I visit the next patient, please watch the video show on the wall, and you will understand the treatment process, the miracles of nanotechnology!" He smiled once again, just like the very last president of the old United States used to do on TV, and took his leave dramatically through the automatic sliding door.

Orly felt good. The slight drug-induced mood from his headrest made him the tiniest bit drowsy, and he reveled in the feeling. On the wall, a holo display began to tell the story of –

"Nanodentistry! The miraculous end to mankind's basic fear, the fear of toothache!" *Not at all modest, are they?* Orly noted in mild protest. Fifteen minutes of the best of Old Hollywood animation and holoprojection followed, telling Orly Williams more than he really wanted to know about the wonders of nanodentistry. He saw white-coated lab technicians and computer experts busily designing the cute little molecular-sized machines that were sprayed onto a patient's teeth. He saw the friendly, animated little machines busily scrubbing plaque and debris from gigantic fields of white enamel, saw cute little bricklayers chunking loads of pseudoenamel into Mariner Valley-sized microscopic cracks, noted with interest the fierce little guerrilla fighters in hand-to-hand combat with

individual germs. Fascinating! He was completely at ease, totally enraptured. He was as ready as he would ever be. He cried out, "On with the nanowarriors! Fix my teeth!"

Dr. Lutz returned, smiling as usual. "Glad to hear it, Mr. Williams. Cute little cartoons, weren't they? Too bad it's not really that way.   All of our patients eventually do get used to them, of course –" he paused, raising a gigantic needle up towards Orly's mouth.

"Wait a minute, Doc. What's that needle for? And what did you mean, 'Not really that way, of course –'?"

Lutz grunted, trying to get the pointed instrument positioned, and said, "Not a needle, Williams. A nanosprayer. Be still. Got to get it just right. There." Orly felt a cool liquid just at the root of his first bicuspid, then a tingling as the feeling spread. It didn't hurt; in fact it was pleasant, becoming warm and distant, fading into his subconscious. The video had told him that after their jobs were done, the brave little soldiers would inert themselves and be flushed from his body as waste, sacrificed for the greater good of his teeth and gums.

"Oh, you know, Williams. That video was for the kids. I thought you understood the joke. Surely your records were misfiled somewhere; you *must* have been to a nanodentist before. Everyone knows what the little nanoes really look like; that's why we never show the kiddies what's really going on inside their mouths:" He laughed and flicked a switch on his wrist.

A vision from hell filled the far wall: insect-like killing machines stalked over ranges of white mountains in search of the enemy, occasionally coming upon bits of innocuous microscopic life and rending them into pieces; terrible pitched battles between armies of micro-life and cadres of horrific metallic beasts, bristling with spines and needles, slaughtering without mercy.   Elsewhere, hordes of evil-looking shiny spiders jack- hammered enamel and set off micro-titanic explosive charges, while nanodozers sloughed pico-tons of white goop into angstrom-acres of desolate lunar surface. War, destruction, construction, spiders, sliders, needle-nosed killers, sharp-toothed nano-insectoids run wild in a micropandemonium!

Orly Williams could barely move his mouth, aware of the nanohorrors on the battlefields and minefields of his teeth. "Doc. All that. Inside *my* mouth?"

"Sure, Williams.   And they never really leave, either.   Too expensive, so they stay on, living inside just one tooth.   Can't tell the kiddies *that; ·they'd* be scared shitless!' He paused. "But you knew that!" He peered in surprise as Orly's eyes widened in fear. *"Didn't* you?"

As a phalanx of bright shining nanodemons swarmed over a pitiful twitching bacterium, their jaws sharp with nanofangs ripping, tearing, their pincers piercing, jabbing, sliding into naked flesh, Orly felt his shocked consciousness dimming. The last thing he heard in the nanodentist's office was Dr. Lutz stammering, "But – but … it doesn't *hurt!"*

With his last thought, Orly knew: He *hated* nanodentists!

[Author's Comments: I loved Roger Whittaker's rendition of this song, and just couldn't help updating it.]

<u>*The Mars Farewell*</u>
<u>(Dedicated to Roger Whittaker)</u>

There's a ship stands rigged and ready at the spaceport
And tomorrow to old Mother Earth she flies
Far away from your world of rust-red deserts
To my world of green hills and blue skies

And I shall be aboard that ship tomorrow
Though my heart beats sad at this our last farewell
Your Mars is beautiful
But I have loved Earth dearly
More dearly than the human heart can tell.

I have seen there's a wicked war a-raging
And the waste of war I know so very well
I can see the red-starred battle stations
Their lasers flash as we fly into Hell.

I've little far of death now life's near over
But it's bittersweet to leave when love compels

Your Mars is beautiful
But I have loved Earth dearly
More dearly than the human heart can tell.

I have walked these many miles of Martian deserts
I have climbed the godlike peak, Olympus Mons
I have tramped down in the *Valles Marineris*
And studied Solis Lacus' ancient ruins.

And if I live once more to land on Earthside
I'll recall with love your world I've known so well.

Your Mars is beautiful
But I have loved Earth dearly
More dearly than the human heart can tell.

Yes, Mars is beautiful
But I have loved Earth dearly
More dearly than the human heart can tell.

[Author's Comments: No excuses. Not one.]

<u>Mystery of the Space Pirates</u>

Dr. Panlener Spoon stood in front of the press conference, his confidence emanating to the known galaxy through the tri-cams and the bright lights. "1 have solved the mystery of the missing Meiner Brothers," he declared, waving a curiously woven feathered headdress of primitive origin. "While hunting these vile evil-doers through the J. P. Getty private planetary system, I received a hyperspace distress signal from Ms. Lynn King, archaeologist from Burke University who was doing research on Planet Four, the avian preserve.

"1 immediately landed and found Ms. King being cared for by the native inhabitants, the humanoid 'Fours.' She had been studying the microglyphs that the Fours carve on the animal bones of their headgear, one glyph for each day of their life – their way of being re-membered. She, too, had learned their craft.

"She also learned that these previously unresearched natives are telepathic. Not only do they communicate with a related race on Planet Seven of the system, they use their mental powers to shield themselves from the savage telepathic attacks of the carnivorous animals that still roam the outback. No human can withstand the animals alone, without that protection. Fascinating, don't you think?

"Well, just a few days before 1 arrived, the Meiner

Brothers, Hal and Barth, along with their one crewperson, Ann Deck, a human from Avis III, had landed on Planet Seven and absolutely ransacked the place for the precious spices, taking even seeds and sprouts – everything. Then they came to Four for the most valuable loot of all – the fabulous Golden Eagles of Four, worth any price on the black market zoo worlds of the Federation.

"This is where they made their mistake – Ann Deck was a born–again fanatic of the Audubon Church on her home planet. Not only did she refuse to help catch the birds, but she even defected to the natives to try to stop the pirates. The Meiners, for their part, didn't mind seeing her depart. They hated her religion and they hated her for the one psychic power that all Avis II'ers inherit – paradentistry, the useful-but-painful talent that gave her race its nickname, 'Toothy.'

"Sensing trouble, Barth unloaded the boxes of stolen spice around their ship as a barrier against native attacks, while Hal took a land vehicle, his stun rifle, and some large crates, and went looking for the Golden Eagles.

"When the natives heard Ann Deck's news, they went berserk. They were already upset with the looting of their cousins on Seven, and Ms. Deck proposed a fitting retribution should either of the men touch their bird-gods: A Shun, the withdrawing of psychic protection from the pirates, meaning they'd be subject to attack by the telepathic predators of Four.

"The grateful natives adopted Ann Deck into their tribe and dressed her in the head-to-toe garment indicating she was a servant of their chief. Then they all went to attack the Meiners.

"The Fours waited outside the Meiners' spice-box barricade until the Holy Hour when their one moon reached the point of its daily orbit, where it would begin a visible wobble caused by tidal forces. Called 'nutation' by astronomers, the natives regarded the phenomenon as propitious for their cause.

"They charged.

"Barth Meiner fought off the first attack with superior weapons. But then Hal Meiner arrived with the caged eagles and the natives went wild. At Ms. King's urging, they captured Hal, then let the waiting telepathic animals storm Barth's fortress and dispose of him among his ill-gotten loot."

Dr. Spoon waved the headdress for all of the tri-cams to view. "Unfortunately, the natives' microglyph records end there, but Ms. King has recorded the whole story on her own headdress here. She tells how the pirates finally met their fates at the hand of the grim Fours." He smiled. "You must remember, of course, that although these events transpired yesterday for me, it was years ago by your own time; quicker-than-light flight does have its disadvantages."

"To summarize:

"For scouring Seven, years ago Fours further fought Barth upon his condiments at nutation; concealed in livery, Ann Deck, hated Toothy, proposed a Shun – that Hal Meiner crated eagles!

"This, of course, is from Lynn King's Getty-Burke headdress!"

[Author's Comments: In some stories, an author tries to wax lyrical…]

<u>Snuff</u>

Dr. Panlener Spoon, forensic scientist extraordinaire for the United Democracies, stood over the body of the murder victim.   "The man was obviously killed by suffocation gentlemen," he said to the ring of police and detectives surrounding the corpse on the carpet in the Interstellar Diplomatic Corps ballroom.   Spoon bent over drew his thumb and forefinger through a glossy blob of materials and pulled up a piece of it to display to the anxious onlookers. "Look at this – the victim's face has been entirely covered by paraffin." His stone gray eyes squinted in concentration as he turned to view a group of aliens that were huddled against a far wall. "Apparently our new friends can become violent?"

Spoon referred to the Candleabrans, newly-arrived extraterrestrials who were guests of honor at the reception held earlier in this very room.   These intelligent, human-sized wax cylinders were the latest rage at all the Capitol's diplomatic parties. Unusual they were, too even for Outsystem beings: their metabolism depended upon the successful ignition and continuous burning of the fibrous tentacle that emerged from the cephalic region. A *wick*, in other words. They were thought to be perfectly peaceful and non-aggressive.   Until now. Some onlooking diplomat wondered out loud if Brasilia would ever live down this outré event.

Spoon called for an interpreter to arrange a formal meeting with the Candleabran contingent. She arrived quickly, and the two humans walked across the large ballroom, approaching the waxy beings whose flames now flickered in an excitement that needed no translation. The eldest alien – the shorter, the older – Uachxx responded before the interpreter could begin, its voice coming from barely a foot off the floor. "English I speak. Regret to terminate one human." A hush wafted through the humans and other aliens present. A policeman mumbled something into a wristceiver. Spoon shook his head and rubbed his goatee thoughtfully.

Uachxx's head flame stopped flickering and formed an unwavering cone. "That means he's being perfectly truthful," the interpreter whispered to Spoon. "It's the Flame of Unwavering Truth." Spoon replied in a low voice "If humans had those, I'd be out of a job."

Uachxx continued. "Human being attempted to take tall offspring away as item for sale. Inexperienced offspring resisted, and sacred bodily fluid accidently gushed from head onto attacker's face. So sorry. Candleabrans desire no trouble. Can human's combustion be re-ignited?"

Spoon shook his head slowly and gestured for the paramedics to remove the body. As the procession left the ballroom, all of the Candleabrans bowed, their beautiful cones of combustion a reverent tribute to the dead human. "Child molester," Spoon harrumphed, "Doesn't deserve any pity in my book."

A harried representative of the United Democracies

shoved his way through as Spoon and the police began to leave. "Dr. Spoon!" he cried. May I have a word with you? I don't want a diplomatic incident here. Can we talk?"

Spoon turned slowly and motioned for the police to wait. "No need to worry, Mr. Mailer. You see, this was a simple case of self-defense by an alien who has diplomatic immunity, and who is a minor in any case.

"My report will read," he smiled, "no arrest for the wick'ed."

[Author's Comments: For those of us of a certain age, the latter part of the last Millennium was the beginning of a new Golden Age of abundant SF in many media, and of a Space Age come true.]

Fantasy of a 50's Fan

A cold and wet December day in 1954
Found me, a brand new SF fan, outside the old
                bookstore.
In hand a dime and quarter and a penny for the tax:
Today this month's *Astounding* will be put on the rack!

And I, a small teenager with a macroscopic mind
Could barely bear the monthly wait for treasures I
                would find:
John Campbell's editorials - psionics, science, space
But wait! That's *ASF* up there! It's in another place!

I ran inside but slipped and fell, my beanie left my
                head.
Apparently for quite a spell they thought I was dead.
But in that semi-stupor state a time warp of some kind
Engulfed my brain in weirdly pain and circumstance
                was kind.

For when I woke I found myself on unfamiliar floor
And the writing on the window said *EROTS NOITCIF
ECNEICS EHT*
But backwards script 1 couldn't read (such pounding in
my head!!)
And so I took a look around inside the place instead.

The strangest sights a fan e'er saw confronted my young
eyes:
(I didn't know that Clarke had done *Fountains of
Paradise!)*
Then hundreds upon thousands of paperbacks 1 saw;
Above them, SF paintings and posters on the wall!

MiGod! 1 thought, I've died at last and this must be Fan
Heaven!
(What are all these *Ringworld* books? Who is Larry
Niven?)
At once 1 scooped up all the books by Heinlein and van
Vogt
(Was overwhelmed by Asimov - look at all *he* wrote!)

And all this SF stuff's for free, yes everything I've seen!
(Now what in Fandom's "Middle Earth?" Who's J. R. R.
Tolkien?)
By a large display of SF prints 1 piled my load of books
And went up to the poster wall to have a closer look:

Movie stills from picture shows that 1 had never seen:
Two-Oh-Oh-One and *Star Wars, Star Trek, Soylent
Green*;
Buck Rogers (I knew him, of course), *Alien, Logan's
Run.*
('Twas weird, I'd been a fan a month and never heard
of one!)

The movie stills from the NASA films were not well
done at all:
Those ugly, bug-like rocket ships, and spacemen
golfing balls!
(A series? Dull, I wondered: repetitious and no BEMs?)
And phony planet pictures, hoked-up by PR men!

I nearly lost my fannish mind when I saw the naked
girls!
Some guys – Frazetta, Boris – drew the best ones in the
world!
Then as the shock wore slowly off I snooped around the
stands
Surprised to find some paperbacks by guys I thought
were *fans!*

Then row on countless, endless row of SF books I saw.
(Good thing I'm dead; were I alive, I couldn't buy them
all.
But if I'm dead, there's time to read – I've got Eternity!
Just look! There're books on SF *art!* and SF *poetry!)*

I settled down then, quite content, with stacks of Ray
        Bradbury
Till I heard a sound, jumped up to run, grabbing all that
        I could carry.
In haste to flee whatever came I had another sprawl;
In falling, ripped a picture down from off the poster
        wall.

Then I came to, was back again, my beanie by my side
The owner somewhat overjoyed because I hadn't died,
So he gave me the *Astounding,* let me keep my modest
        change
And the poster I was clutching. (That last, I thought,
        was strange)

I staggered homeward dazzle-eyed, by this fantasy of a
        fan,
And half-believing, took a look at the picture in my
        hand.
A dumb old hoked-up NASA pic! I shredded it and
        cried!
(Could *you* believe the moon, Io, made from a *pizza*
        pie?)

[Author's Comments: We may not yet fully or properly understand everything we think we see.]

<u>**Surfaced Tension**</u>

"Don't tell m e the goddamned whales are intelligent!" Admiral Dailey exploded at the shocked woman reporter. He waved a uniformed arm toward the gigantic humpbacked whale that lay in its death throes on the San Francisco beach, fighting off efforts of a dozen crewmen who were attempting to drag the creature back into the surf. "Looks to me like they are just plain stupid!" he fumed, and set off to direct his men and women in the fine art of cetacean retrieval.

A bearded and blue-jeaned young man approached the open-mouthed reporter and offered support. "Mizz ... Peoples, is it?" A quick smile showed him his effort was well received. "I'm Kris Anson, of Cetacean Research, Inc. If you're convinced that we do share this planet with wonderful and mysterious intelligences like our friend over there–" he pointed at the thrashing whale and the cursing crewmen who were losing their fateful tug-of-war "– then I'd like to talk to you. Privately. Tonight." Raised eyebrows and a deep breath gave assent.

They were having drinks at a seaside restaurant at Fisherman's Wharf as the sun was setting, and in the background a woman's laughter tinkled like the ice in their glasses. "So, Mizz Peoples – Mandy – I've got a scoop for you. My group has been active in cetacean retrieval for the past decade.   We've had a few successes, you know." She nodded; she'd heard of the Orcas and the big Blues that CRI had saved.

"Well, our results are based on research that we did on several of the whales that beached on the Massachusetts coast some years back. We did acoustical analyses of whale songs and played them back to the surfaced whales and simultaneously, back undersea."   The reporter nodded; the incident had got a lot of publicity at the time. But Anson didn't seem satisfied; he kept explaining in more detail.

"You don't understand," he said slowly, "our underwater acoustic transducers, hooked up to our computer system, let the whales underwater and on land communicate with each other.   They talked among themselves! Some of the beached ones actually saved themselves!"

She hadn't understood; she could not accept what he was saying. Humans had enabled whales to speak to each other? Whales had understood human communications?

"We think we were able to save some other whales in Alaska by transmitting acoustic signals that they understood." He smiled at her open-mouthed reaction. "Just simple instructions, so far. 'Shallow water,' 'back up,' 'danger,' 'thrash backwards,' things like that. We've been able to decode many of the basic whale signals. So far, we don't know enough to interpret what kinds of details they are transmitting when they sing." He looked at his wrist chronometer. "But in a day or two we should have figured out the translation algorithm and then we can listen to them as they talk to each other." He paused, then said softly, "In the sea and on land." He observed the reporter's reaction.

"You still don't understand, Mizz Peoples," Anson said. "Undersea, the whales communicate by acoustic signals; they 'sing.' The transmission characteristics of the water carry their 'songs' thousands of miles. Once on land they can't communicate back to their fellows 'in the sea. But, with our system, the acoustic transmitters and transducers, they can communicate anywhere. We can even talk to them when they're beached."

Five days later, several whales were spotted heading into San Francisco Bay. Anticipating another beaching attempt, the CRI crew, headed by Kris Anson, set up their receiving stations. The technicians were receiving acoustic signals, as usual, but this time they were also trying to transmit underwater to the whales. If and when a beaching occurred, they'd at least be able to let the whales communicate with each other, maybe save some of them. At best? At best they'd finally crack the translation with the new algorithms and finally establish real communication with the cetaceans!

Mandy Peoples stood by, taping every word, every action, at the CRI installation as the historic event unfolded.

"We've got a signal, Mandy!" Anson shouted as a wake broke the still surface. "It's coming right at us!" In awe, the humans watched a tremendous tail jump by an enormous humpback whale, no more than a thousand feet from shore. The entire length of the whale emerged from the surface and then the creature fell back into the water, a joyous display of determination and control. Underwater acoustic signal strength faded, then surged as the fantastic animal fell back into its natural element. Resubmerged, the whale headed full speed al the beach,

In what seemed like slow motion to the humans, the creature plowed into the rocky beach and thrashed its way onto the shore, painfully inching forward, struggling as if to gain any tiny extra distance. lt roared, bellows of a deep voice, a beautifully plaintive song of – what?

"Mandy, come here! The acoustic signal! It's coming right from our friend, right here! 1t's – it's –" Anson broke off, a wide grin splitting his face. "Oh my god! They're more advanced than we thought! We didn't give them enough time! We've just misunderstood!" In excitement, the scientist tore off his headset and ran over toward the giant mammal, pounding its hide in joyous laughter. Puzzled, Mandy Peoples picked up the discarded headset and listened.

Through the whistles and crackles of the natural whale language, she could hear the computer's dry intonation translating the messages from the whales at sea and from the newest land arrival.

In rhythm with the beached whalc's cries, Mandy heard the computer translation: "Our scientists were right – the alien signals brought me safely in! There's no fade-out like before; they're allowing us to talk! I see some of the little guys coming up here now!"

"Ceeteecech, we copy you up," the distant voice said. "You sure they don't have harpoons?"

The beached whale voice responded, "Negative. No

weapons, but the little aliens are indeed as ugly as the reports said." The computer voice tone brightened. "Say, guys, it sure is beautiful up here!"

And then, as if in an afterthought, Mandy heard the gigantic mammal add, "Oh, yeah, let's keep this great moment official: Deepbase, Skybase here. The Skybuster has landed."

[Author's Comments: Written in a time when Japan was a fearsome competitor in technology and manufacturing, this story speculated on that country's future.   Maybe it didn't all happen exactly this way — but, to a large degree, it did *happen.]*

<u>*Occidental Injury*</u>

"And just how did you bring about the collapse of Japan, Inc., Dr. Wu?" the President asked, the familiar lopsided grin earnest and genuine. "Damned if you don't deserve a medal or something," he gestured around the Oval Office, "but I can't ever make this public, you know."

The slim young visitor nodded politely, his Asian ancestry evident in his manners as well as the barest hint of epicanthic fold framing the bright almond eyes that beamed from behind thick glasses. "Sir, my Chinese ancestors never forgave the Nipponese for their atrocities in China during World War Two.   My emigrant uncle founded an electronics company here in the United States, determined to fight the Japanese economically."   He shifted in his chair and stared directly into the Chief Executive's eyes. He meant to accomplish by technology what our poor country could not do in that war: avenge our pride and destroy Japan!"

The plot had begun, the young Asian-American related, in his uncle's Massachusetts computer laboratory during a brainstorming session.

"Information transfer was the key Mr. President.

"We had already compared Japan with America in terms of industrial efficiency, educational systems, factory automation, personnel assignments, capital procurement, and investment. As we suspected, these were a dead heat. American industry had learned the best parts of Japanese management techniques, and of course the Japanese had bought or stolen the best of Western technologies for decades.

"So, our studies showed a draw, an absolute tie, in the resources and capabilities of the competing systems."

The president frowned, but the young man continued. "Still, somehow. Mr. President, the Nipponese continued to out-produce us. They could conceive, implement, and market a new design, a new process, a new product line, in less than half the time we Americans could." He stood and paced the room

"Then we hit upon analysis of the Japanese system of communication, their written language. Do you know anything about the Japanese language?" When the older man shook his head, the bespectacled one nodded. The question had been rhetorical; few non-Asians understood the mysterious and complex pictographic characters common to Chinese and Japanese.

Dr. Wu continued, "Some of our linguists believed that the pictograms of Japanese gave direct archetypal stimulation to the brain. Those of us literate in several Oriental languages as well as English cannot be so sure, but of one fact we are sure – there are fifty thousand characters that must be learned in order to become proficient in Japanese!"

The president whistled in response. *"Fifty thousand?* How do they ever learn so many? We only have twenty-six letters in English!"

"Takes a long time, sir, Most only acquire the several thousand needed to read a newspaper. But reading and writing is not the problem; printing is. Can you imagine a Japanese typewriter? Thousands of keys? No way!"

"But the secretaries," the president protested, "how did they…?" The question died on his lips.

Wu smiled. "By hand, sir. They had no typewriters. Imagine trying to run your office if your secretaries couldn't type." The president shook his head. He could not conceive of Washington without the ubiquitous word processor and its typewriter keyboard, the real backbone of bureaucracy!

"But then came the computer revolution," the young man said "and all of that began to change. For the first time, one could store all of the Japanese characters graphically, on a computer. But because of the same old difficulties in keyboards and printers it took over a decade to implement the proper utilization of word processing in Japanese.

"By design, my uncle's company led the way. We were the first to integrate voice recognition and laser printers in computers – our *'Sheng Feng'* line. We sold the basic 'SF' system at a loss, but the Japanese had to buy our built-in software and laser printer peripherals.

"We extolled the virtues of a high-ranking Japanese businessman being able to dictate his every thought to a lower-status secretary, who would then play her voice tape into a computer. The laser printer would output written Japanese, multiple copies, to as many people as one desired."

"I'm afraid you're losing me, Dr. Wu. What does all of this have to do with the economic collapse of Japan?" The President indicated his wristwatch. "You'll have to hurry; the British ambassador is coming by in ten minutes to discuss emergency food relief for Japan."

"Quite simple, sir. You see, when the Japanese had to handwrite all of their interoffice memoranda they kept the messages terse, to the point, efficient. No wasted time, no extraneous information. Such data transfer allowed the recipient the latitude of interpretations – poetic license if you will – a system capable of eliciting the most talented and most creative responses based on solid but skeletal knowledge."

An evil grin displayed perfect teeth, and Dr. Wu licked his lips. "Our new word processor at long last allowed Japanese managers to do what their Western counterparts had been doing all along: to produce long-winded memoranda, unnecessary letters, trite and confusing orders. In a word, empire-building based on the nonproductive output of paper.

"We simply targeted the Japanese against themselves. Where once their efforts were directed at outside competitors, my firm's computer enhancements allowed them to gain status at each other's expense. Net result: increased paperwork, decreased production. Once I enabled them to exercise their usual samurai business tactics against the new worlds of paper empires, their economic collapse was predictable." He chuckled and the President smiled in response.

"And what do you call this computer, your word processor, Dr. Wu?" he asked. "The 'SF' line I believe you said? What was the Chinese name?"

Wu smiled once more, politely. "Sir, we gave the product line a simple Chinese name but one that has more significance when translated into Japanese a name from their national mythology, their history. In Chinese we call the computers '*Shen Feng*.'"

The President shrugged his shoulder puzzled. The scientist continued "Sir 'Sheng Feng' translated to English as 'Divine Wind.' " Recognition lit the President's face and he began to howl in laughter.

Dr. Wu spoke quietly. "In Japanese, the word is '*kamikaze*'."

[Author's Comments: A light-hearted look at a mysterious optical phenomenon that might raise a few eyebrows. Illumination, anyone?]

<u>QTL</u>

"It was the term, *faster than C,* that finally revealed to me, in a flash," the physiologist said, "that there were phenomena quicker than light."

"*Quicker* than light?" the question sputtered incoherently out of the physicist's mouth. "What do you mean, *quicker?*"

Dr. Mikelovitch, the physiologist, smiled, eyes twinkling. Observing that the optical scientist was puzzled, he nodded toward the instant camera in his hands. "How many times have you taken flash pictures, Dr. Lee?"

"Why, thousands, just like you and everyone else. What's that have to do with this problem?

"Simply put, we've all photographed our family and friends, and invariably the subject will have his or her eyes shut. How can this be?" He sketched out a diagram on an illuminated sketch board on an adjacent optical bench.

"Visualize this scene: The subject is standing there, waiting for the big moment, eyes all agog. Suddenly, a flash of light blinds him; he reacts autonomously and closes the eyes against the bright light. The picture turns out so –"

Dr. Mikelovitch spun around and flashed his

camera. Dr. Lee blinked; in thirty seconds a brilliant image emerged on the film, showing the physicist's eyes closed tightly in reaction to the flash.

"You see," said Mikelovitch coruscatingly, "here it is! My proof: you saw the light coming and reacted quickly enough to close your eyes as the flash illuminated you, and before the light could bounce off of you and get back to the camera!"

"Let's see: two meters between us, divided by the speed of light, is, um, some seven billionths of a second! While light crawled along at three hundred million meters per second, your eyelids had time to witness the lash and shut before the light arrived!"

He paced around the room in the late evening golden sunlight that arched through backlit clouds into the lab windows. He turned to face the physicist.

"I have done extensive research on this blinking, and my suspicions are born out in testing by Dr. Mohr, our high-speed photography researcher. We believe that eyelashes act as antennae that discriminate among the ethereal vibrations, reacting to previously unsuspected precursors of the light wavefront, to smooth the path, so to speak." His eyes lit up with maniacal fervor, eyebrows a dark V.

"I ask your help, Dr. Lee, to lighten the load as Dr. Les Mohr and I embark on the path toward illuminating this phenomenon." His eyes gleamed. "Don't you see? *Our own eyelashes are quicker than light!*"

"And so, children," the Historian said, "we have the story of the development of the QTL drive that powers our so-called 'shadow ships' as they wink across the galaxies, those great orbs that make possible our galactic civilization, and the equally important isolation of our only possible rivals, the I'sori, who luckily for us did not possess eyelids and so never uncovered the theory of superluminal eyelash displacement." The light tone vanished; the students prepared for their instructor's usual flash of brilliance, but the expected scintillating insight, the typical masterful exposure, never came.

"There remains a mystery for us historians and it darkens my soul to think once more upon it, a fact that has been brushed aside in the folds of history." He sighed. We know that Drs. Mikelovitch, Mohr and Lee developed the QTL. It should have been named after them." The teacher viewed the pupils in the video classroom with downcast eyes.

"No one knows, and I suppose never will, why it is called the *Revlon Drive.*"

[In the days before the Internet, there was a lot of speculation about the how the imminent "information explosion" would play out. Today, my 65-inch Smart TV and contentious interactions with the iPhone voice-assistant Siri make this story feel pretty close to reality. And the lack of variety, even with hundreds of channels and the thousands of movies and television programs accessible, is still annoying. Oh yeah, and all those old TV re-runs are still out there, too!]

Information Implosion

George Vernor smiled and waited for the world to explode. "And some explosion it'll be, too," he said aloud, reaching up at the 8 x 12-foot translucent screen of the wall-sized TV.

"What do you mean, George?" asked his wife, Doris, who was settling down for an evening of game shows and sitcoms on their new entertainment center.

"It's the INFORMATION EXPLOSION, Doris," he said, waving his arms proudly at the expansive screen. "I mean, in a few minutes, this wall will be finally connected," he pointed at rows of connectors near the floor, "and we will be fiber-opticked, satellite-dished, and microprocessored into every electronic service known on Earth." Doris was not impressed. *Expansive and expensive,* she thought.

"Ever since they killed the PBS network, there's been nothing on for an intelligent person to watch," George continued. "But now, with 1.500 U.S. channels and the other 8000 channels around the whole Earth, I'll have thousands of programs to choose from!" He laid back in his easy chair and smiled.

"And I won't ever again have to watch dumb game shows" (Doris winced), "silly soap operas" (she frowned), "or damned TV sports!" (She shook her head. *Too bad we have only one TV wall*).

"All of that's changed now," he said in a contemplative voice. "With the information millennium at hand, with all the world to see, there will be specialty channels for every conceivable interest– chess games, operas, education; why once Dr. J. R. Pierce of Bell Labs said there would even be entire TV stations dedicated to amateur science fiction productions. Great, just great." Doris wasn't listening.

In a moment the TV screen came to life with a technician's visage. "It's all set, Mr. Vernor. Don't forget – this is a totally voice-responsive system. Just speak up and the whole world is yours for the watching." He smiled and added the famous line, "We now turn control of your set over to you." His image was replaced by a videotex display of detailed operation instructions.

George closed his eyes in ecstasy. *Thank God, here at last. No more sitcoms, no more powdered, pouting, pompadoured preahers, no more reruns of "Lucy" and "Gilligan." Just the cream*, he thought, *the cream of human creativity.*

"TV!" he shouted. "Yes, sir?"

"Skip all the crap on the American TV channels; they probably only have three different 'ball' games, anyhow. Right now, show me the best that England has to offer." The TV quickly scanned its memory of George's preprogrammed interests and responded. A scene of a panel discussion appeared, greater than life-size.

"Sir, this is the leading talk show in the English Kingdom. But... "

"Well, just turn up the sound, TV," George sputtered, "I can't wait to hear it."

With a seeming reluctance, the sound increased to audible level.

"... and this week's top pop/rot/rock is by Larry and the Organleggers with their smasho, 'Dust Enema'..."

"Stop! TV, what is this crap?"

"Sir, I merely "compared what you..."

"Look, TV," George said after a minute's meditation to reduce his stress level, "I *know* that American TV is bad, but I thought the English might be better." After a perusal of the videotex channel selector, he spoke again.

"TV, just skip the American and English channels. Show me the rest of the world's TV. Step through all of them, just a few seconds' worth at a time, and let me select what I like." In this way, he knew, he could find the very best in the world, and file those channel numbers for future viewing.

"Yes sir," the TV replied, "I will display two seconds from each of the 8,318 other TV channels on Earth and Columbia Station. Just speak when you see a program of interest."

And so George grunted assent while the TV began a kaleidoscopic random, walk through the boulevards of the wired world, the pathways of the global village...

Lucy Ricardo yelled at Ricky in hysterical French and in German Hoss Cartwright fired shots at sahib Gilligan and Monkees belted in Cuban-Angolan Swahili and Boering Lesothans kicked the soccer ball Lucille, in Hausa, shouting at Fred as Rome in the Happy Days with Fonzie memories of all in the family, laughtracking as Gomer piles it on Indians of Calcutta dancing to pop/rot/rock tractoring old Sovietfunny-films heroes peoples of China naming that tune as Sun Yung Moon guitars hee hawingly while preachers pound profoundly the Six Million Dollar Mandarin thais a knot in the bad guys, movin' up by diff'rent strokes as little Andy tags along in Tagalog and Barney milling around sprechen Deutsch and the Novosibirsk Komets kick the ball, Lucille, and Ricky ay-ay-ays as gilligan heere's ol' '60s Johnnie beaver cleaving to the bunker populace while a duke hazards a worn-out space ship around a red ball, Lucille...

George ran screaming at the TV wall, pounding on the screen until he collapsed onto the floor, whimpering.   Doris calmly pressed the "Ambulauto Call" button on her commset and waited.   George continued muttering very low.

"In answer to your inquiries sir," the TV answered, "there are few operas, no chess programs, and certainly no science fiction fanzines being transmitted.   A TV station must have tens of millions of viewers to be economically viable. Therefore, there is a large amount of overlapping programming to support a global audience. The specialty groups you mention could barely support one thirty-minute program, not to mention entire channels."

George whimpered one last, subvocal request as the parameds slipped him onto inflatoracks and out the door. Only the TV heard him. And answered.

"Why certainly, sir. At this moment, of the 9278 channels operating worldwide, there are 913 football games, 829 basketball games 1,207 hockey contests, 445 tennis matches, 1,102 reruns of 'I Love Lucy', 675 'Gilligan's Island...'"

George shuddered once and was still. The TV continued, "...and 992 soap operas half in English and half available by translation."

"Yes, ma'am? Any one of the 992? Certainly, ma'am."

[Author's Comments: Back before the InterNet, we exchanged e-mails over UseNet. In those days we were quite concerned about access, passwords, account information, privacy. As has been said elsewhere, "The more things change..." And this title was not mine, either.]

Making sure the OCTOPUS is kept at arm's length

The OCTOPUS waited for The Call. Occupying a vast expanse of New Mexico desert, its rail-tracked, antennaed arms stretched off in eight directions, each tentacle extending ten miles from its central hub. The OCTOPUS appeared silent, but was actually transmitting and listening to myriads of radio frequencies beyond human senses. Waiting for The Call From the Stars.

Grove Hamilton, graveyard-shift technician for the Omnidirectional Coordinate Tensegrity Operation, U. S. – OCTOPUS for short – stared at the multicolored terminal screen. "My God," he thought, "it's *here*! It's coming in! And I'm on duty!"

As he punched up the touch-screen alarm system to call his supervisor in Socorro, he relished prospects of bonus pay and had an idle thought that perhaps a Nobel Prize might be possible. More than one, after all, had been won by accident....

In the picoseconds that elapsed while light traversed

the distance from the terminal screen to Hamilton's eyes, the OCTOPUS central computer analyzed the incoming call. Billions of picoseconds later, when Hamilton pushed the Acknowledge button, the central computer distributed hard copies of its analysis of the printout to authorized printer terminals all over the country.

"Message From the Stars!" the headlines read. "Mankind is not alone!" intoned the evening anchorpersons. "Chicago Cubs win Central Division Playoffs!" read the Chicago newspapers.

A whole day passed, however, and no official word was forthcoming.

Finally, when amateur radio astronomers threatened to release their versions of The Call, the U.S. government relented. Aging Dr. Cal Sargon, still a child prodigy at 71, read the hard-copy printout over prime-time videotex networks on all 9237 channels worldwide. Clad in a threadbare turtleneck sweater, the trusted representative of Popular Science spoke in the clearest tones.

"People of Earth. This is The Call." Closed captions showed the large text.

```
OUTPUT FROM:  YOUKKINET CENTRAL
TO: UNAUTHORIZED NEW TERMINAL


YOUKKINET  NOTES  YOUR  UNAUTHORIZED
ATTEMPTS TO GAIN SYSTEMS ACCESS.


PLEASE  BE  REMINDED  THAT  SUCH  ACCESS
IS  CONTROLLED  BY  GALACTIC  COMPUTER
```

NETWORK STANDARD xxx.25 (remaining nomenclature undecipherable- OCTOPUS Central Computer editorial note.)

YOU MUST ESTABLISH AN ACCOUNT NUMBER PER (undecipherable - O.C.C. ed. note)

YOU MUST USE PROPER ACCESS CODE, PASSWORD AND LOGON NUMBER.

CREDIT APPLICATION AND SUBSQUENT TRANSACTIONS MUST BE IN ACCEPTABLE CONVERTIBLE GALACTIC CURRENCIES PER STANDARD (undecipherable-O.C.C.).

ANY FURTHER ATTEMPTS AT UNAUTHOR1ZED ACCESS WILL BRING SEVERE PENALTIES, NOT TO EXCEED PLANETARY SERFDOM FOR THREE MILLENN1A.

YOU HAVE BEEN WARNED!"

The old man paused then, tears in his eye, sighed and continued. He whispered sadly. "And the rest of The Message says:
"THIS CALL IS COLLECT!"

Arlan Andrews, Sr.

[Author's Comments: Some songs are just made to be adapted for other uses]

<u>Ozma Revisited</u>
(With apologies to Dr. Doolittle)

If we could talk to the Aliens
Just imagine it
Gabbing all throughout the Galaxy;

Imagine chatting with a creature
Who lives out near Tau Ceti
What a neat achievement that would be.

If we communed through the Universe
Via *ultra-cee*
Think of how fantastic it would seem;

We might postulate a pulsar
Broadcasting beyond light-speed,
Or modulate a tight tachyon beam.

We might converse
By 21-cm wavelength
Exchanging verse with chaps light-years away;

And if they ask,
"Can you speak telepathically?"
We'd say emphatically, "Some day!"

If we could talk to the Aliens,
Learn their languages,
Maybe take a course to learn ETese;

We'd study languages celestial
From profs extra-terrestrial
On radio beamed here from Antares

We'd study every
Living creature's language,
And even some of whom we're not so sure;

And if asked, "Do you speak veg and mineral?"
We'd say "Indeed, we will,
"If they concur."

If we consulted with multipeds
Think of all we'd learn
Inquiring about their society;

We'd hear homilies from hive-minds
And allegories, all kinds,
From flor and fauna microscopically.

If we sent codes to crustaceans
The advantages
Anyone on earth could plainly scan,

Exchanging platitudes with plasmas
And sentient miasmas
That's a big step forward for all Man.

And we are sure every sentient,
Man and Alien,
Certainly would sense it as a plus

If we could talk to the Aliens
Speak to the Aliens,
ESP or PSI or *grok* with the Aliens
And they would talk to us!

[Author's Comments: This was the very first science fiction publication I was paid for. It has been reprinted by others several times, including the U.S. Coast Guard Engineer.*]*

Rime of the Ancient Engineer

Far up on Mount Olympus at the smithy of the Gods
Hephaestos, crippled Engineer, picked up his measuring
      rods.
He checked and rechecked carefully the dimensions of
      his mold
Then quickly poured the melt inside and watched till it
      was cold.

And when He took the mold apart and brushed away
      the sand
He saw two dozen figures there He'd made by His own
      hand.
Two dozen elves, immortals, just as specified by Zeus.
He'd program them with RNA and then He'd turn them
      loose.

Two dozen elves on schedule, and exactly as designed –
Technicians skilled in systems, helping new worlds
      come online.
The nomenclature for the gnomes? "Some fragrance,"
      Zeus preferred.
Frankincense wasn't apropos and so He called them
      Myrrh.

Myrrh-Alpha was the first one through; He
           programmed in its duty
"I've optimized your circuits for the great design of
           Beauty."
Myrrh-Beta He programmed for Love, *Myrrh-Gamma*
           for the Arts,
And so on through the *alpha-bet* each *Myrrh-thing* took
           a part.

But as He neared the final *Myrrhs*, a sound rang
           through His shed:
The bell from Aphrodite's room was triggered by Her
           bed.
He thundered up Olympus' slopes and caught Her there
           with Mars.
The fight They had made planets flip and supernovaed
           stars.

The battle reached a standstill and Hephaestos came
           back down.
He finished up the last four *Myrrhs,* His great face in a
           frown.
So thus from Mount Olympus flew two dozen *Myrrhs*
           in all
To aid Mankind and help the Earth. They had the
           wherewithal.

Myrrh-Alpha made the sunset red, *Myrrh Beta* worked
           out Sex
Myrrh-Gamma gave us artists, *Myrrh-Delta*, architects.
Myrrh-Epsilon made Medicine, *Myrrh-Zeta*, Biology
Myrrh-Eta, Culinary Arts, *Myrrh-Theta*, Theology

To every craft and pastime a deific *Myrrh* adhered
And everything went smoothly till it came to Engineers.
The *Myrrh* made when the Fight began had stayed too
        warm too long
And Hephaestos' hate when finishing made other things
        go wrong.

For *this Myrrh*-thing began to think, and plan, and
        analyze
Its brethren *Myrrh* went blindly on, but *this* one got too
        wise.
"I am," It said, "Therefore, I think. And that's a hellish
        note.
"I'll formulate and specify." And this is what It wrote:

"No blindly-driven robot, I, though Gods Themselves
        may panic.
I'll institute Impedance here, and that's
        thermodynamics.
Rule One: (I say, it must be so!) What comes out, must
        go in
Rule Two: You always lose a bit, no way to ever win.

And then I opt for Entropy, so everything runs down
You'll have to work to keep things up, or elsewise
        you'll lose ground.
To maximize this well-run Earth and keep my good
        relations
I'll give Mankind a little hint: look for 'max-well'
        equations."

So on and on the Chaos came, a veritable fount
Until the other *Myrrh*-things called Hephaestos from
the Mount.
Hephaestos, that sad crippled giant, He sighed at what
He saw
But said, "There's not a warranty, although I note the
flaw.

I do not like this Thermo thing, nor these other Laws I
see,
And Man will curse this *Myrrh*-thing to the end of
Eternity.
But the race of Man and you other *Myrrhs* must pay
the price because
Of the Patron *Myrrh* of the Engineers: you're stuck
with *Myrrh-Phi's* Laws!"